Freesemann

THE TURKEY GIRL

A ZUNI CINDERELLA STORY

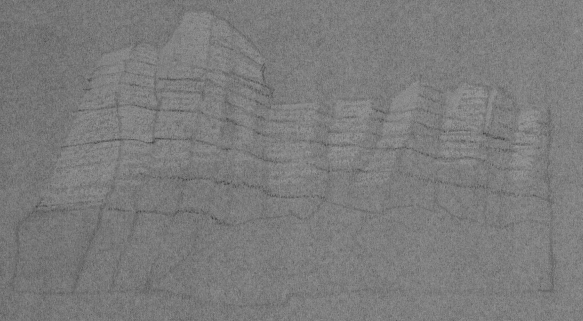

Retold by **Penny Pollock**   Illustrated by **Ed Young**

Little, Brown and Company
Boston New York Toronto London

First Edition

Library of Congress Cataloging-in-Publication Data

Pollock, Penny.
The Turkey Girl : a Zuni Cinderella Story / retold by Penny Pollock ; illustrated by Ed Young. — 1st ed.
   p. cm.
Summary: In this Indian variant of a familiar story, some turkeys make a doeskin dress for the poor girl who tends them so that she can participate in a sacred dance, but they desert her when she fails to return as promised.
   ISBN 0-316-71314-7
   1. Zuni Indians — Legends. 2. Cinderella (Tale) [1. Zuni Indians — Legends. 2. Indians of North America — New Mexico — Legends.] I. Young, Ed, ill. II. Title.
E99.Z9P65 1996
398.2'089'974 — dc20
[E]   93-28947

10 9 8 7 6 5 4 3 2 1

SC

Published simultaneously in Canada
by Little, Brown & Company (Canada) Limited

Printed in Hong Kong

The drawings in this book were done in oil crayon and pastel.

For our son Jeff, who loves the earth
P. P.
*To true sincerity
in oneself and then to the world*
E.Y.

AUTHOR'S NOTE

Like many Americans, I have the blood of more than one race flowing in my veins. My mother's family was English. My father's family descended from Chief Tarhe, a Wyandotte Indian. In the early 1900s, the United States government offered each Wyandotte family a small lot on Mount Rainier if they would forgo living on a reservation. My family accepted this offer. Although it is only a symbol, I treasure that piece of land.

When I came upon the story of the Turkey Girl, I was struck by how different it is from the European version — the Cinderella story my English grandmother told me. That story ended with Cinderella's wedding to the prince. In contrast, the various Native American versions end with the hard truth that when we break our trust with Mother Earth, we pay a price.

I am grateful to Frank Hamilton Cushing, who traveled to New Mexico in 1879 to study the Zunis. Cushing came to admire the Zunis so much that he not only moved in with them, he became a member of the tribe. Among his many contributions is his collection of Zuni folktales, which is where I found "The Turkey Girl."

In the days of the ancients, a young girl lived alone in the shadow of Thunder Mountain. Her small mud-walled hut nestled against the edge of the pueblo village, Matsaki. The other houses rose above hers, piled atop one another, with ladders to reach their roof doors.

The young girl was so poor she herded turkeys for a living. The turkeys belonged to the wealthy families of Matsaki. They valued the black-and-white tail feathers of the huge birds for decorating prayer sticks and ceremonial masks. The wealthy families cared little for the orphaned herder, calling her the Turkey Girl and paying her with corn and cast-off clothes.

Each dawn, as Sun-Father began his long journey across the sky, the Turkey Girl, clad in her tattered dress, threadbare shawl, and yucca-cactus sandals, led the turkeys from Matsaki. Ducking her head to avoid the wind-blown desert dust, she walked across a dry arroyo, through the Canyon of Cottonwoods, and up the cliff of Thunder Mountain to graze the turkeys on the flat-topped mesa.

Every evening, as Sun-Father returned to his resting place, the Turkey Girl led her beloved turkeys back to their stockade of cedar sticks.

"Good night, my friends," she would say as she latched the gate. The turkeys, although used to her talk, never replied.

The young girl faithfully tended her [...] over them through the hot sum[...] ered piñon nuts from the wind-tw[...] she said good night to the turkeys, t[...] chipped water jug to the spring. Other girls goss[...]

The Turkey Girl knew they would not talk with her[...] her fit company only for turkeys. She held her head high[...] did not mind. She was balancing her filled jug on her head w[...] the herald-priest appeared on one of the flat housetops. Everyone grew quiet.

"Hear me, children of Sun-Father and Earth-Mother. In four days' time, before the harvest moon, the Dance of the Sacred Bird will be held in Hawikuh. It is fitting that you attend."

Murmurs of plans for the festival rippled through the crowd near the spring.

The Turkey Girl caught the excitement, imagining herself danc-ing with the others. Rich odors of the feast would rise from the fires. A pulsing beat would fill the air. Dancers in bright colors would circle together. . . . Water from her jug sloshed onto her tattered shawl, ending her daydream. She had no place at the dance. She was just the Turkey Girl, clad in rags.

But she could not stop dreaming of attending the dance. She spoke of little else. The turkeys were her only listeners, but they listened well, for she had always been loyal to them.

On the day of the dance, the villagers left in the crisp dawn for Hawikuh. The Turkey Girl and her turkeys left for the plains below Thunder Mountain. Tears streaked the dust on her cheeks.

As she stumbled along, a commotion among her flock drew her attention. She had no sooner turned than a huge gobbler stepped forward, stretched out his proud neck, and said, "Maiden Mother, do not water the desert with your tears. You shall go to the dance."

The young girl sank to the ground and gasped, "How is it that you speak my tongue, Old One?"

"We belong to an ancient race, Maiden Mother, and have many secrets our tall brothers do not know."

The Turkey Girl's smile brought beauty to her smudged face. "I should have understood as much," she said. "I thank you for your generous thoughts, but I cannot go to the dance. The only clothes I own are the rags you see before you."

"If you will follow us, we will tend to your clothes," replied the old gobbler, turning back toward Matsaki.

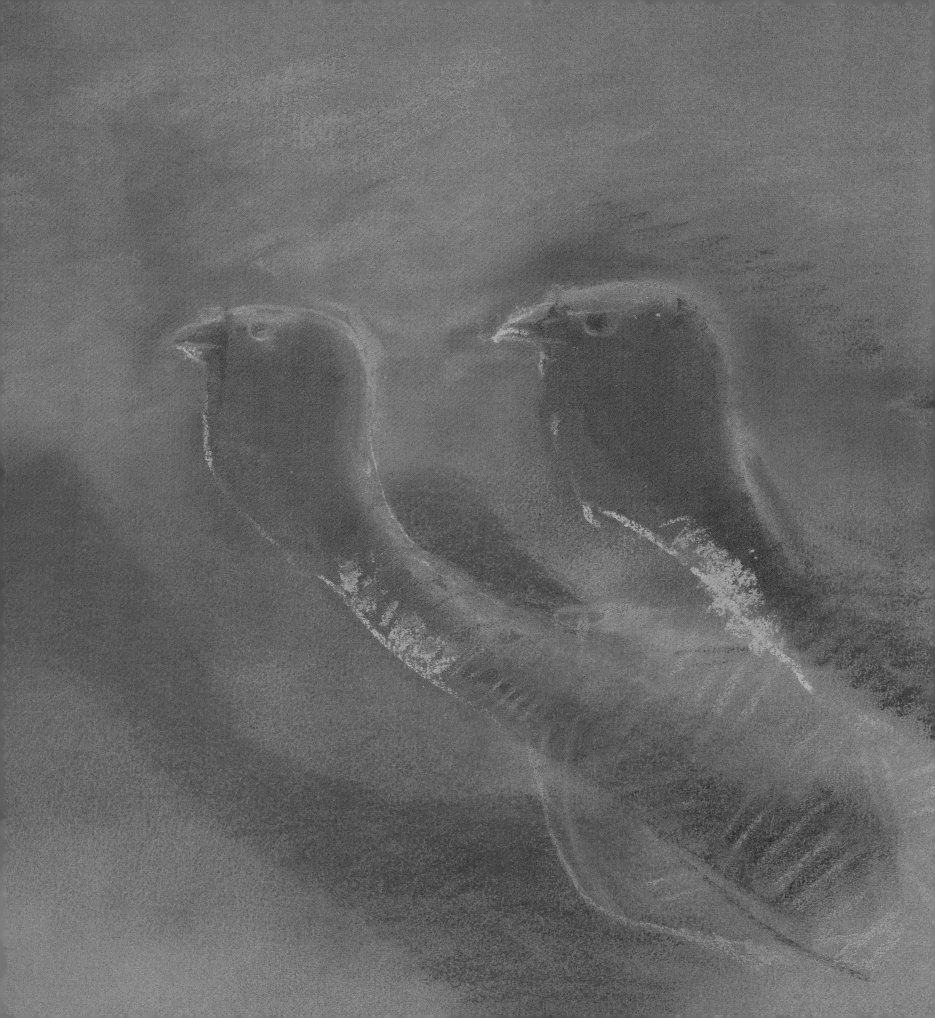

Willingly the young girl followed them straight into their pen.

"Welcome to our home," said the old turkey. Without a further word, he directed the other birds to encircle the Turkey Girl. Breaking into song, with their heads high and their wings fluttering, they danced round the young maiden, dusting her with the soft tips of their wings. Dirt and twigs fell from her black hair, which began to shine like a starlit night. Brighter still glowed her dark eyes.

Satisfied with her cleanliness, the turkeys again encircled the Turkey Girl. With their heads turned away, they fanned out their beautiful tails and entwined their wings to give her a small room in which to undress.

"Lay your clothes on the ground," said the big gobbler.

The Turkey Girl spread her tattered dress and ragged shawl on the ground next to her yucca sandals.

Swaying up and down, the turkeys treaded and tapped new life into her old clothes. They sang while they worked. Their song, a low hum, was accented with the *clack-click*, *clack-click* of their beaks.

Soon the Turkey Girl stood in a white doeskin dress belted with red-and-yellow cloth. Rare shells dangled from its hem. Colored twine and beads threaded her soft white moccasins. Black-and-white turkey feathers edged her dark mantle.

As she gazed in wonder at her clothes, the gobbler spoke once more. "You must have jewels to wear to the dance."

The Turkey Girl smiled and replied, "How could that be possible, Old One?"

The gobbler tossed his head in a superior way. "Have you not noticed the carelessness of our tall brothers?" he asked. "We have collected their dropped treasures for many moons and stored them in our gullets. Now, stand still, for the time of the dance is near."

The Turkey Girl stood as still as the red-and-yellow plains beneath Thunder Mountain. The turkeys flew above her head, circling slowly, gurgling softly as they coughed up treasures. Suddenly they flew faster, and down rained turquoise necklaces and earrings of delicate beauty. Bracelets of silver tumbled after them.

"Now you may go to the dance," said the gobbler in approval. The other turkeys nodded their agreement.

"My . . . my friends," stammered the girl, "how can I thank you?"

"We ask no thanks," replied the gobbler. "You have given us much. We wish to repay your kindness. All that we ask is that you not forget us. For if you do, we will understand that you are mean of spirit and deserve the hard life that is yours."

"Forget you?" answered the girl, looking down to finger her silver bracelets. "I could not."

"You will prove that by returning to us before Sun-Father returns to his sacred place."

"I will do as you ask," replied the Turkey Girl. She shifted her fine mantle from shoulder to shoulder, admiring its richness.

"And while you are gone, the latch of our cage will remain unlocked," added the gobbler.

"Why do you wish that, Old Father?" The Turkey Girl wriggled her feet, anxious to leave for the dance.

"If you break your word, we shall seek our freedom. If you return in this day's sunlight, all shall be as before."

The girl hastily agreed to his request and ran down the river path that led to Hawikuh. When she saw her reflection in the water, her excitement grew. Her beauty matched that of the desert in bloom. Now everyone would see she was fit company for more than turkeys.

When the Turkey Girl reached Hawikuh, she raced through the long covered way that led to the plaza. People were already dancing in a circle around the musicians and the altar.

The throb of drums, pulsing in the heart of the plaza, was accented with a jangling-clacking sound. Peering from behind the crowd, she saw that the sound came from the turtle-shell rattles encircling the arms and legs of the dancing braves. The sound of the rattles reminded her of the turkeys' song.

Gathering courage from this memory, she stepped forward.

The musicians, setting the rhythm with their flutes, drums, and notched sticks, missed a beat when they saw her. Her beauty was so great, everyone stopped to stare. Who was this stranger? Where had she come from?

The musicians began again and so did the dancers, although they still turned to watch the Turkey Girl. With a smile as shining as her long hair, she joined the dance.

Braves, wearing feathered masks, pressed close to dance near her. The music thrummed with power. The dancers echoed the beat with their pounding feet. Sun-colored dust floated from the hard-packed earth. Round and round the dancers flowed like a sinuous snake as Sun-Father, high above the plaza, looked down.

The Turkey Girl danced every dance, her heart beating in time with her stomping feet. At last she was among the proud maidens and handsome braves.

But she did not forget her turkeys.

As the sun's rays slanted gold across the plaza, she said to herself, *When the music quiets, I will run to my turkey friends.*

No sooner had the music died than it sprang back to life. The Turkey Girl danced on.

Fingers of darkness reached across the plaza. *I will leave this minute*, the young girl told herself. But then a brave brushed against her, and she began to wonder how it was that she should leave the festival for mere turkeys. Were they not just gabbling birds?

In time, Sun-Father's afterglow softened the earth. Shadows of evening chilled the Turkey Girl. Her steps slowed as she remembered the turkeys' kindness to her and her promise to them. She broke from the ring of dancers, ran across the plaza, under the covered way, and down the river path to the turkey pen.

It stood empty, its gate creaking in loneliness.

"My friends!" cried the Turkey Girl, running through the purple of nightfall to the top of Thunder Mountain. "Wait! I am here!"

The turkeys had waited until Sun-Father fell asleep behind the mountain. Then, seeing that she had broken her trust with them, they had left Matsaki and their Maiden Mother, never to return.

Great was her sorrow at their silence. Greater still was her sorrow when she saw by moonlight that her fine dress had become rags, her shawl tatters, and her sandals worn yucca fibers. Then she understood that she had lost her turkey friends forever.

From that day unto this, turkeys have lived apart from their tall
brothers, for the Turkey Girl kept not her word.
Thus shortens my story.